Siva

INDIANA

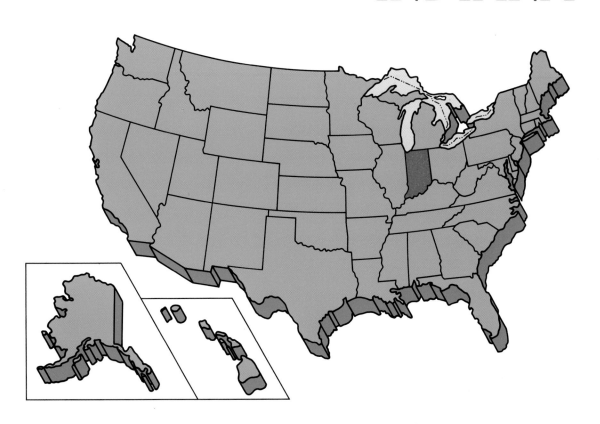

INDIANA

Gwenyth Swain

Lerner Publications Company

LIBRARY OF CONGRESS
CATALOGING-IN-PUBLICATION DATA
Swain, Gwenyth.
      Indiana / Gwenyth Swain.
          p.   cm. — (Hello USA)
      Includes index.
      Summary: An introduction to the geography, history, economy, people, environmental issues, and interesting sites of Indiana.
      ISBN 0-8225-2721-9 (lib. bdg.)
      1. Indiana—Juvenile literature.
   [1. Indiana.]   I. Title.   II. Series.
   F526.3.S93   1992
   977.2—dc20   91-20621
                                          CIP
                                           AC

Cover photograph by Maslowski Photo.

The glossary on page 69 gives definitions of words shown in **bold type** in the text.

Manufactured in the United States of America

1 2 3 4 5 6 7 8 9 10 01 00 99 98 97 96 95 94 93 92

 This book is printed on acid-free, recyclable paper.

CONTENTS

Did You Know . . . ?

☐ Most of the stone used to build the Empire State Building in New York City came from a hole in Indiana. In the early 1930s, the Empire Hole near Oolitic was full of limestone, a stone often used in building skyscrapers. Workers dug out enough limestone to fill a train more than 400 flatcars long. In all, 200,000 cubic feet (5,669 cubic meters) of Indiana limestone went into making the Empire State Building.

☐ No one knows the exact origin of *Hoosier*, the nickname for people from Indiana. Poet James Whitcomb Riley has an explanation, which may or may not be true. In pioneer times, says Riley, Indiana was a rough place. After a terrible fight in a bar, one man looked on the floor. He asked, "Whose ear?," and the state's nickname was born.

☐ Indiana's capital was almost named Tecumseh, after the Shawnee Indian who lived in Prophetstown, Indiana, in the early 1800s.

☐ The first pay toilet in the United States opened for business in 1910 at the Terre Haute, Indiana, train station.

A Trip Around the State

Many travelers only glimpse the state of Indiana from the window of a car, truck, or bus. Roads crisscross the state and lead south to Kentucky, north to Michigan, east to Ohio, and west to Illinois. Highways also give the state its motto, the Crossroads of America. But there's much more to Indiana than roadways. The smallest midwestern state packs a lot of variety inside its borders.

From interstate highways to shady lanes, Indiana lives up to its motto, the Crossroads of America.

Lake Michigan carves a half-circle of land out of northwestern Indiana. Hills along the Ohio River mark Indiana's southern boundary. Between Lake Michigan and the southern hills are farms, limestone quarries, grassy prairies, swamps, and river valleys.

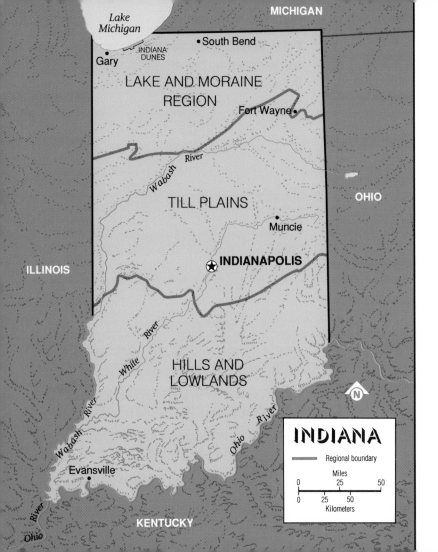

The state of Indiana has three major land areas— the Lake and Moraine region in the north, the central Till Plains, and the Hills and Lowlands region in the south.

Indiana's landscape was shaped by **glaciers,** huge sheets of ice. About 400,000 years ago, glaciers pushed south from the North Pole. During the last **Ice Age,** which ended about 10,000 years ago, glaciers covered the northern two-thirds of what became Indiana.

Melting glaciers carved out many of Indiana's rivers and streams, including the Ohio, Wabash, and White rivers. Indiana's longest river is the Wabash, which flows from near Fort Wayne to the state's southwestern tip.

Wherever the glaciers passed, they left behind **till,** or rich soil. In the northern third of Indiana, they wore the ground down, leaving behind flat plains and piles of sand and rock called **moraines.**

The Ohio River flows along Indiana's southern boundary.

Lakes and streams at Chain O'
Lakes State Park near Fort Wayne
were formed thousands of years
ago by melting glaciers.

Some water from melting glaciers gathered in pools to form
swamps and lakes in northern Indiana. Lake Wawasee, Lake Maxinkuckee, and many other lakes
dot the area. This part of the Hoosier state is known as the Lake and
Moraine region.

Central Indiana's plains offer good ground for farming.

Central Indiana, called the Till Plains region, was also once covered by glaciers, which scraped the land smooth. The region's flat plains are some of the richest in the country for farming.

13

Mist rises over the rolling hills of southern Indiana.

The southern third of Indiana was untouched by glaciers. Because glaciers did not enrich the soil, land in this part of the state generally is not ideal for farming. Hills, steep ridges, deep valleys, and caves are common. The area's name—the Hills and Lowlands region—comes from the ups and downs of its hills and valleys.

For thousands of years after the glaciers melted, prairie grass grew in northern Indiana, while dense forests covered the rest of the state. Settlers cleared most of Indiana's trees for farming, but some forests have since grown back.

Each spring, dogwood, tulip poplar (the state tree), and rosebud trees bloom. More color fills the forests each fall when leaves on oak, maple, and beech trees turn shades of yellow, red, and orange-brown.

Dogwood berries brighten Indiana's forests in the fall.

15

A bobcat watches from a treetop perch.

White-tailed deer, raccoon, and skunks live in the woods of southern Indiana. Bobcats prowl the state's more remote forests.

Indiana's summers are often warm and humid, with temperatures averaging 75° F (24° C). Lots of rainfall—about 40 inches (102 centimeters) per year—and a long growing season make Indiana a good place for farming and gardening.

Winters can be cold, windy, and snowy in the north. Southern Indiana's winters are milder and sometimes very rainy. Northern Indiana receives an average of 40 inches (100 cm) of snow compared to southern Indiana's 10 inches (25 cm). In January, Hoosiers living in Evansville often enjoy temperatures 10 degrees warmer than their northern neighbors in South Bend. Overall temperatures average 28° F (–2° C) in midwinter.

Ice sparkles near a lighthouse on Lake Michigan.

Spring flooding happens almost every year in some low-lying areas around the state. Tornadoes and severe thunderstorms are common in spring and summer. In winter, ice storms can make travel treacherous. As Hoosiers often like to say, "If you don't like the weather in Indiana, stick around. It won't be long before a change."

17

This building at Angel Mounds, near Evansville, is based on structures built by Mississippian Indians 1,000 years ago.

Indiana's Story

Humans first came to what is now Indiana in about 11,000 B.C., when ice from glaciers still covered parts of the state. These people lived by tracking and killing deer and elk with spears.

At first people moved often, following the animals they hunted. Some of these people, known as Woodland Indians, began building villages about 2,000 years ago. Woodland Indians buried their dead inside large, log-lined pits covered with mounds of earth. Their houses did not survive, but some of their burial places can still be seen at Mounds State Park near Madison, Indiana.

A Native American woman demonstrates basket weaving at Angel Mounds.

More than 1,000 years ago, Mississippian Indians moved north into what became Indiana. These Indians used wood and clay to build temple mounds shaped like pyramids. The people farmed, fished in nearby rivers, and hunted deer and other wild animals.

At one time, 1,000 Mississippian Indians lived in Angel Mounds, a town on the Ohio River near present-day Evansville. These people abandoned their towns about 400 years ago. Experts still don't know why the Mississippian Indians left the area.

Miami, Potawatomi, Shawnee, and Delaware Indians moved into present-day Indiana beginning in the late 1600s. Many had been forced from their homes in the east by wars or by European settlers.

The Potawatomi and Miami were Indiana's biggest Native American groups. They lived in small villages made up of bark-covered houses. Near their towns, they planted melons, beans, pumpkins, and corn. They also hunted deer for food and used the skins for clothing.

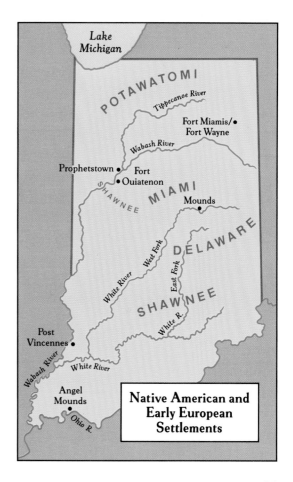

Native American and Early European Settlements

In the mid-1600s, French priests and fur traders may have met these Indians when they visited what became Indiana. The French explorer La Salle was the first European known to have traveled through Indiana. In 1679 Miami Indian guides led La Salle and a group of French adventurers south from Quebec. Quebec was then the capital of New France, France's empire in North America.

La Salle set up fur-trading posts along rivers and streams in what became Indiana. The Frenchmen who lived at the posts learned Indian customs, and some married Indian women. The French traded metal pots, guns, and knives for

La Salle

furs gathered by the Indians. France grew rich on the fur trade.

Great Britain was also eager to make a fortune in the fur trade. To protect their trade and their land from the British, the French built three forts—Post Vincennes on the Wabash River, Fort Miamis at

At Historic Fort Wayne, people in costume now welcome visitors from around the state.

what is now Fort Wayne, and Fort Ouiatenon near Lafayette. The French also made agreements with Native Americans in the area. Together, the Indians and French would fight against the British.

But forts and agreements were not enough to save France's empire. In 1754 Great Britain and France went to war. This conflict, called the French and Indian War, ended in defeat for France by 1763. Only the names of towns such as Vincennes, Terre Haute, and Lafayette remain to remind us of Indiana's French past.

After the war, the British won control of the fur trade and most of North America, including the land that later became Indiana. But the British didn't keep either for long.

Great Britain ruled several **colonies** on the eastern coast of North America. People living in the American colonies had grown tired of being governed by the British. In 1775 the American colonists began fighting a war to win their independence, or freedom.

Most battles in the American War of Independence, or Revolutionary War, were fought in the eastern colonies. But the British also planned to attack the American colonists from the western frontier, which at that time included Indiana.

Major George Rogers Clark, on the American side, thought that the best way to stop a British attack from the west was to attack the British first. In 1778 Clark captured Fort Sackville, a British fort in the old French town of Vincennes.

With a small band of volunteers, George Rogers Clark trudged through swampy ground to capture a British fort at Vincennes in 1778.

Clark's expedition was one of the most important western battles in the Revolutionary War. After several more years of fighting, the American colonists won their independence from the British. In 1783 they formed the United States of America.

By capturing settlements such as Vincennes, Clark helped the Americans claim a great deal of land that the British had controlled. Clark and his men were rewarded by the new U.S. government with land in what became Indiana Territory.

Indiana Territory was created by the United States in 1800. The territory included all of present-day Indiana, Illinois, and Wisconsin, and the western half of Michigan. Fewer than 3,000 white settlers, most of them fur traders or former French colonists, lived in all of the territory.

William Henry Harrison was appointed governor of the new territory and arrived in the territorial capital of Vincennes in May 1800. New settlers began moving into

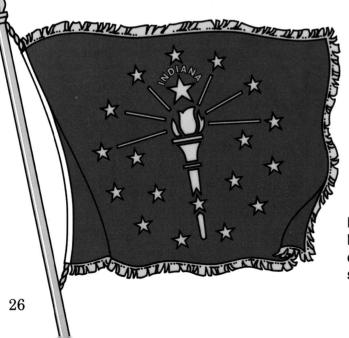

Nineteen stars and a liberty torch fill the flag of Indiana, the nineteenth state in the Union.

the territory from nearby states.

Soon Indiana's white residents were ready to draft a **constitution,** the first step toward becoming a state. On December 11, 1816, Indiana became the 19th state in the Union.

During Indiana's first 30 years, Native Americans were forced to give up much of their land. Indians still living in the state found it harder and harder to survive as white settlers cleared old hunting areas. In 1830 the U.S. government began sending the Indians remaining in Indiana to new homes, called **reservations,** in other states.

In the hot summer of 1838, the last group of Native Americans left Indiana. Nearly 850 Potawatomi were forced to march across

Before being forced to leave Indiana in 1838, hundreds of Potawatomi Indians lived in camps like this one at Crooked Creek.

Indiana, Illinois, and Missouri to a reservation in Kansas. So many Indians died during the journey that the Potawatomi still call this march the Trail of Death.

Tippecanoe and Tyler Too!

This catchy campaign slogan helped elect a president in 1841. What does the slogan mean?

It all goes back to 1811, when William Henry Harrison was governor of Indiana Territory. Harrison met with many Native Americans to get them to sign treaties that would take away their land. Tecumseh, a Shawnee Indian, argued that Harrison's treaties weren't legal.

Tecumseh believed that the land belonged to all Native Americans. No single Indian or tribe, Tecumseh said, could sell land or sign a treaty.

Territorial Governor Harrison first met Tecumseh in 1810.

People at this political gathering in 1841 knew that "Tippecanoe" was just another name for William Henry Harrison.

Tecumseh asked all Indians—even longtime enemies—to join him in saving their land. Tecumseh's followers gathered at Prophetstown, a settlement in Indiana Territory near the Tippecanoe and Wabash rivers.

Harrison called Tecumseh a "bold, active, sensible man." But Harrison also decided that Tecumseh was dangerous.

In 1811 while Tecumseh was away, Harrison and his troops marched toward Prophetstown. Word of Harrison's approach soon reached Indian leaders. Early on November 7, Native Americans from 14 tribes attacked Harrison in the Battle of Tippecanoe. Both sides lost many men, and finally the Indians retreated. When Tecumseh returned to Prophetstown, his supporters had scattered and Harrison was claiming victory.

People remembered Harrison's role in the Battle of Tippecanoe when he ran for president in 1841. "Tippecanoe" became the former governor's nickname, while "Tyler Too" referred to John Tyler, who served as Harrison's vice president.

Not all settlers came to Indiana to farm or to escape slavery. Settlers came to New Harmony, on the Wabash River, in 1825 to try to change the world. The nation's first preschool, first trade school, and first public library were all founded in this progressive Indiana town.

More and more white settlers moved to Indiana after the Indians had been removed. Some settlers came because slavery was against the law in Indiana. Others came to help build canals and roads. But most of the new settlers came to farm.

30

Abraham Lincoln grew up in southern Indiana on Little Pigeon Creek.

Thomas Lincoln and his family moved to the state in 1816 and were typical of Indiana's settlers. Tom's young son Abraham spent most of his childhood in and around the family's windowless log cabin on Little Pigeon Creek.

Young Abraham worked hard to help his father clear land and plant corn. There was little time left for him to go to school. During the 14 years Abraham lived in Indiana, he spent only 12 months in a classroom.

31

In 1861 volunteers prepared to leave Indiana for Civil War battlefields.

Thirty years after leaving Indiana, Abraham Lincoln was elected president of the United States. President Lincoln found the country deeply divided over the question of slavery. Many Southerners thought slavery was necessary. They lived on large farms, called **plantations**, and depended on African-American slaves to work in the fields. Many Northerners were opposed to slavery. They thought that no person should own another person.

When the two sides couldn't agree, 11 Southern states left the Union and formed the Confed-eracy, a separate country that allowed slavery. In 1861 the Confederacy and the Union began fighting the Civil War.

Indiana stayed in the Union, but people in the state didn't agree about slavery. Slavery was against the law in Indiana, but many set-

By the mid-1800s, Indianapolis was a bustling city.

tlers who had moved there from the South were not opposed to using slave labor. These Hoosiers were used to slavery. Many had slave-owning relatives and friends in the South.

Nonetheless, on the day when President Lincoln called for troops to support the Union, 10,000 Hoosiers signed up. No battles were fought in Indiana, but nearly 200,000 of the state's troops helped the Union defeat the Confederacy.

After the Civil War ended in 1865, African-American slaves were freed and had the right to live wherever they wanted. Many moved to cities such as Indianapolis to find jobs.

33

Children at the Gary Public Library in the early 1900s proudly showed their ethnic backgrounds.

Immigrants, settlers from foreign countries, also came to the state to work. In 1906 the U.S. Steel Corporation built a huge factory and a city, called Gary, for its workers. During the early 1900s, immigrants from eastern Europe poured into the new city. African Americans also came to work in the city's steel plants. In less than 20 years, Gary was the sixth largest city in the state, and steel was one of Indiana's most important industries.

34

Steelworkers and other factory employees in the early 1900s often worked 12-hour days, seven days per week. These long hours troubled Eugene V. Debs, a young railway worker from Terre Haute, Indiana. Debs wanted to improve workers' lives. Along with shorter hours and better pay, Debs wanted workers to own the companies where they worked.

Debs created the Socialist party to try to pass laws that would help workers. Although Debs was not always successful in achieving his goals, many of the things he fought for—such as the 8-hour workday —have since become law.

Eugene V. Debs

By the 1920s, life for most people in Indiana was easier than it had been in pioneer times. More Hoosiers lived in cities where they could enjoy electricity and other conveniences. Many people owned cars and drove to new state parks. Hoosiers went to movie theaters and joined bicycling and hunting clubs for fun.

Car-owning Hoosiers in the 1920s couldn't always go where they wanted, because there were so few good roads.

Many Hoosiers joined the Ku Klux Klan in the 1920s.

But many white Hoosiers worried about the African Americans who came to Indiana looking for work. Some white Indianans complained that black people were taking jobs away from them.

Nearly 240,000 Hoosiers joined the Ku Klux Klan in the 1920s. The Klan was a group for white people only. Members believed that white people and black people should not mix.

Klan members also disliked new immigrants who came to Indiana from Europe for better jobs. The Klan thought native-born Americans should be hired first.

Some members of the Klan acted as if laws did not apply to them. The Indiana Klan elected a new leader, D. C. Stephenson, in 1923. Stephenson was a popular speaker but he was also a troubled man who sometimes became violent.

In 1925 he attacked a white Indianapolis woman and held her hostage. Before she died from her injuries, the woman was able to testify against Stephenson. By the end of the 1920s, Stephenson was in jail and Hoosiers had deserted the Klan by the thousands.

D. C. Stephenson

Hard times and high prices hit Indiana and the nation during the Great Depression of the 1930s. People throughout the state lost their jobs when banks failed and businesses closed. Thousands of Hoosiers left farms in the country to look for scarce factory jobs in Indiana's cities.

As Indiana's economy grew stronger after the Great Depression, more companies located in the state. By the 1960s, Indiana was the most popular state in the nation for companies wanting to build new factories. Indiana's location—at the Crossroads of America—made it a good place to do business. Goods could be shipped cheaply and companies could make better profits in a state like Indiana, with its good transportation system.

Workers in the 1950s helped make Indiana a center for new industry.

11,000 B.C. ★ First humans arrive in what is now Indiana

A.D. 900 ★ Mississippian Indians live along the Ohio River until about 1600

1679 ★ French explorer La Salle travels through Indiana

1778 ★ George Rogers Clark's troops capture Fort Sackville

1811 ★ Battle of Tippecanoe

1816 ★ Indiana becomes the 19th state in the Union

By 1990 about 91,000 miles (146,000 kilometers) of roads and highways crisscrossed the state. The Indiana that Abraham Lincoln knew—with log cabins and endless forests—is gone. Nowadays more Hoosiers live in cities and suburbs than in small towns or on farms. But despite these changes, Indiana remembers its past and faces its future with typical Hoosier pride.

1906 1911 1920   1988

U.S. Steel builds Gary steel mills

First Indianapolis 500 race

For the first time, more Hoosiers live in cities than in the country

J. Danforth Quayle is elected vice president of the United States

J. Danforth Quayle
(left) **of Huntington, Indiana, was sworn in as vice president of the United States in 1989.**

41

Fireworks light up the Indianapolis skyline.

Living and Working in Indiana

If you had never seen or heard anything about Indiana aside from its name, you'd probably expect to find many Indians in the state. After all, *Indiana* means "land of the Indians."

Native Americans outnumbered whites when Indiana became a state, but they make up less than 1 percent of the 5.5 million people now living in the state. Where did the other 99 percent come from?

These Amish girls are descendants of Germans who came to Indiana in the 1800s.

Most were born in the United States. Nearly 90 percent of all Hoosiers are white Americans of English, Scottish, Irish, and German backgrounds. Many of their ancestors left homes in Kentucky, Tennessee, and Ohio to settle in Indiana in the 1800s.

African Americans make up almost 8 percent of the state's residents. Another 2 percent of people living in Indiana are of Spanish-speaking backgrounds.

Most people in Indiana live and work in cities and towns. Indianapolis is the state's largest city, with over 700,000 people. Other big cities include Fort Wayne, South Bend, Gary, Muncie, and Evansville.

Indianapolis, the state capital, is where Hoosiers go to make their opinions known to the state government and to enjoy city life.

45

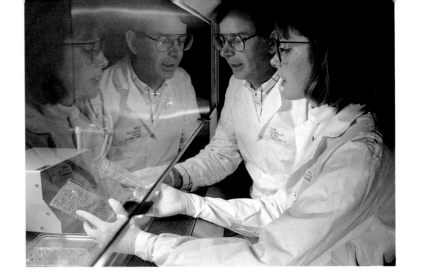

Prescription drugs are a major Indiana product.

Half of Indiana's workers have service jobs, jobs in which people help others by providing some kind of service. Bank clerks, bus drivers, teachers, salespeople, and hotel employees are just a few of Indiana's service workers.

Service jobs in Indianapolis depend mostly on business from conventions and special events. Events such as the Indianapolis 500-mile race, or Indy 500, bring visitors from all over the country to stay in Indianapolis's hotels, eat at the city's restaurants, and spend money at local stores. Thousands of people in Indianapolis work to meet the needs of these visitors.

More than one-quarter of all Hoosiers work in manufacturing. These workers build cars, make car parts, medicines, and steel. In the 1980s, Indiana made less money from steel. Because Indiana's mills cannot always make steel as cheaply as mills in other countries can, many steelworkers in Gary, Hammond, and other Indiana cities have lost their jobs.

In the 1800s, most Hoosiers farmed, but nowadays only 5 percent work in agriculture. Indiana's farmers grow large crops of corn and soybeans. Many also raise hogs for bacon and pork, and chickens for their eggs.

Pigs *(left)* **enjoy a good wallow in the mud at a central Indiana farm.**

47

Racer John Andretti makes a pit stop during the 75th running of the Indy 500.

When Hoosiers aren't working, they're often playing or watching a game. Sports have long been popular in Indiana.

In 1911 drivers competed in the first Indy 500. Each May since then, thousands of fans have gathered at the brickyard, a nickname for the Indianapolis Motor Speedway that dates back to the days when the track was made of brick.

In the first race, winner Ray

Harroun careened around the track at an average speed of 75 miles per hour (121 kilometers per hour). Nowadays, speeds of over 200 mph (322 kph) are common.

Indiana's basketball players aren't quite this fast, but their fans pack high-school and college gyms. In the same year as the first Indianapolis 500, teams played in the state's first high-school basketball tournament. Indiana's fans go so crazy over basketball that sportswriters call their behavior *Hoosier hysteria.*

One of Indiana University's famous Hurryin' Hoosiers shoots a basket.

**Crispus Attucks's
1955 game**

The Crispus Attucks
High School Tigers

In March 1955, Hoosier hysteria swept through Crispus Attucks High School. Crispus Attucks— named after the first African American to die in the Revolutionary War—was once the only high school for blacks in Indianapolis. The school was built in the 1920s by whites who were afraid to have their children in the same classroom with black students.

Black teens got their own school, but they didn't have the same rights as whites. The Crispus Attucks basketball team wasn't allowed to play in the state basketball championship until 1942. Even then, their gym didn't have bleachers, so every game was an "away" game, held at the opposing team's gym.

Most white Hoosiers didn't think that an all-black team could win the state championship. But in 1955 the Crispus Attucks Tigers not only won, they set a new record for the most points scored in a championship game. The next year the Tigers thrilled fans again with a perfect record of 31 wins and no losses. The Crispus Attucks Tigers fought for—and won—respect on the basketball court.

Nonprofessional sports are especially popular in Indianapolis, which is sometimes called the Amateur Sports Capital of the World. Olympic hopefuls compete at the city's swimming and track facilities. Cyclists train at the Major Taylor Velodrome.

Indianapolis has several professional teams as well. The Pacers basketball club draws fans from all over the state. Since 1984 the Colts have played football at the Hoosier Dome in downtown Indianapolis.

At Conner Prairie Pioneer Settlement, you'll enter 1830s Indiana.

Each year Indiana's towns and cities host a variety of special events. The little town of Beanblossom welcomes bluegrass music pickers for a festival each June. History buffs can travel back in time year round at Conner Prairie Pioneer Settlement near Noblesville.

The Children's Museum of Indianapolis welcomes visitors of all ages. You can watch the world's largest water clock tell time, try hands-on science experiments, or explore ancient Egypt—and meet a 2,500-year-old mummy.

Whether you live in Indiana or are just visiting, you're bound to get a friendly welcome. Indiana is famous far and wide for its "Hoosier hospitality."

53

Protecting the Environment

From farm fields to forests, Indiana's greatest natural resource is its land. Since the early 1900s, Hoosiers have worked to preserve and protect that land.

In the past, protecting the land has often meant working to set it aside in parks. A unique part of Indiana's environment is preserved at Indiana Dunes State Park and National Lakeshore near Gary.

Bess Sheehan was just one of many Hoosiers who helped save Indiana's dunes. When she moved to Gary in 1909, the city was only a few years old. The city's houses and factories were built on flattened sand dunes along the southern shore of Lake Michigan. At first Sheehan fought constantly against sand—sand in her shoes, sand in her food, sand in her house. But soon she was fighting to save the sand from destruction.

Many dunes were leveled to make way for factories.

The sand dunes just outside the city were home to rare plants and animals not normally found in Indiana. The dunes were a special place, and Sheehan was angry that more and more dunes were being destroyed as cities and factories grew.

Bess Sheehan was not alone in her love of the dunes. From 1916 to 1923, she and other local women asked people to sign petitions, organized meetings, and talked to lawmakers. All their hard work paid off when the Indiana Dunes State Park

In the 1960s, the mayor of Gary showed his support for protecting the dunes.

56

opened in 1923. Even more land was set aside in 1966 for the Indiana Dunes National Lakeshore.

People in Indiana continue to preserve some land in parks. They also work to protect the entire state in new and different ways. The population of this smallest midwestern state has been growing steadily since the 1980s. At the same time, space in Indiana's **landfills**—holes dug in the earth for burying garbage—has been shrinking.

Garbage abounds at a landfill in central Indiana.

Curbside bins make it easy to recycle.

Hoosiers threw away about 17,200 tons of garbage each day in the early 1990s. But by the year 2010, people in Indiana hope to bury only half as much trash in their landfills.

How will they meet this goal? First they are looking into the future. Under a new law passed in 1990, Hoosiers must make a plan, through the year 2010, for disposing of their **solid waste,** or garbage. More importantly, people in communities throughout the state are asking themselves how they can cut down on the amount of solid waste they produce.

By creating less garbage, Hoosiers will turn fewer acres into landfills. The solid waste law encourages people to work together to plan how they will use and protect the land around them.

Hoosiers young and old are joining in the search for ways to stop making so much trash. They are learning the four R's—Recycle what you can, Reduce what you use, Reject products that can't be recycled, and Reuse whenever possible.

Indiana's 1990 solid waste reduction law means more and more Hoosiers are recycling.

Many communities are setting up ways of collecting recyclable newspaper, scrap paper, cardboard, glass, plastic, aluminum, and other items. Curbside collection points have handy, self-service bins, one for each kind of product to be recycled. From these sites, materials are trucked to larger recycling centers.

Some of Indiana's companies are working to reduce waste. One company, for example, is developing a collapsible milk pouch. When the empty pouch is punched down, it takes up 70 percent less space than plastic jugs.

Milk jugs, plastic packaging, styrofoam cups, and other throwaways take up a great deal of landfill space. More and more Hoosiers are rejecting products with too much packaging or packaging that can't be recycled. They are also reusing bags, bottles, and other containers more than ever before.

These milk pouches are designed to take up less space in a landfill.

60

Hikers climb the shifting sands of the Indiana dunes.

As people make the four R's part of their lives, they ensure that Indiana's natural beauty won't be hidden under piles of solid waste. From Bess Sheehan to today's recycling volunteers, Hoosiers carry on a long tradition of caring for the land around them.

Indiana's Famous People

ACTIVISTS & LEADERS

Levi Coffin (1798–1877) moved to Fountain City, Indiana, in 1826. Coffin opposed slavery and helped slaves from the South travel North to freedom. The owner of a general store, Coffin refused to sell anything made under the Southern slave system.

Richard Hatcher (born 1933) surprised white politicians in Gary, Indiana, when he was elected mayor in 1967. Hatcher was one of the first African Americans to serve as mayor of a midsize city. Mayor Hatcher was reelected four times.

▲ LEVI COFFIN

RICHARD HATCHER ▶

TENSKWATAWA ▶

◀ RYAN WHITE

Tenskwatawa (1768?–1834), the Shawnee Prophet, was a religious leader for Native Americans. Tenskwatawa moved to Prophetstown, near present-day Lafayette, in the early 1800s. With his brother Tecumseh, he brought Indians from different tribes together in an alliance.

Ryan White (1971–1990) suffered from hemophilia, a blood disease, and was accidentally given blood contaminated with the AIDS virus. In 1985 parents in Kokomo, Indiana, said White could not go to school with their children. Ryan White won his fight to go to school and worked to help others overcome their fear of AIDS.

Jim Davis (born 1945) from Marion, Indiana, is best known as the creator of **Garfield** (birthdate unknown). Thanks to Davis, Garfield, a *very* grumpy cat, has his own cartoon strip and stars in television specials.

David Letterman (born 1947) is a television comedian and host of "Late Night with David Letterman." Born in Indianapolis, he started his career as a weatherman. Letterman once reported that hailstones "bigger than canned hams" were falling.

Twyla Tharp (born 1941) was born in Portland, Indiana, and creates modern dances set to classical, jazz, and popular music. Tharp started her own dance company in 1965.

◀ JIM DAVIS and GARFIELD

TWYLA THARP ▶

▲ DAVID LETTERMAN

◀ LARRY JOE BIRD

MAJOR TAYLOR ▶

ATHLETES

Larry Joe Bird (born 1956) stands 6 feet 9 inches (2 meters) tall and is considered one of the finest basketball players in the game's history. Bird attended Indiana State University in Terre Haute and was named College Basketball Player of the Year in 1979. Later that year he began playing for the Boston Celtics.

Marshall ("Major") Taylor (1878–1932) was born in Indianapolis. Taylor was the world champion bicycle racer in 1899. Because he was African American, Taylor was not allowed to use tracks in many American cities. Nowadays, bike races in Indianapolis are held at the Major Taylor Velodrome.

63

EXPLORER

Virgil ("Gus") Grissom (1926–1967) was the third American to explore space. The Mitchell, Indiana, native died during a practice run for the launching of Apollo I, the first mission to explore the moon.

JOURNALISTS

Jane Pauley (born 1950) grew up in Indianapolis and got her first job there as a television news reporter. She was cohost of "The Today Show" for 13 years before starting her own interview program called "Real Life with Jane Pauley."

Ernie Pyle (1900–1945) was born on a farm near Dana, Indiana. Pyle became a newspaper reporter and covered World War II. In his articles, Pyle focused on the lives of ordinary soldiers instead of generals. He was killed by enemy fire.

◀ JANE PAULEY

ERNIE PYLE ▶

HOAGY CARMICHAEL ▶

▼ THE JACKSONS

MUSICIANS

Hoagy Carmichael (1899–1981) began writing songs as a student at Indiana University in the 1920s. His slow and haunting melodies include "Stardust" and "Georgia on My Mind."

The Jacksons of Gary are Indiana's most famous musical family. **Michael** (born 1958) and **Janet** (born 1966) are two of the world's highest paid singers. Michael's 1982 album *Thriller* sold more copies than any previous recording. With brothers **Tito**,

64

Jermaine, **Jackie**, and **Marlon**, Michael first performed with the Jackson Five in the 1960s. Sister **LaToya** also has a successful music career.

John Mellencamp (born 1951) was born in Seymour, Indiana, and is known for his blend of pop, rock, and country music. In songs such as "Pink Houses," Mellencamp tells the story of poor Americans living in small towns.

OUTLAW

John Dillinger (1902–1934) terrorized the Midwest during the early 1930s with daring bank robberies and shootings. Captured and jailed in Lake County, Indiana, Dillinger escaped using a fake pistol carved out of wood. A few months later in Chicago, FBI agents gunned Dillinger down.

▲ JOHN MELLENCAMP

◀ JOHN DILLINGER

WRITERS

Kurt Vonnegut, Jr., (born 1922) is a native of Indianapolis. He has written best-selling novels including *God Bless You, Mr. Rosewater* (which takes place mainly in his hometown), *Slaughterhouse Five*, and *Cat's Cradle*.

Jessamyn West (1902–1984) wrote books based on her upbringing in Jennings County, Indiana. In *Massacre at Fall Creek* she tells the true story of nine Indians murdered by white settlers. The settlers were put on trial in Pendleton, Indiana, in 1824. This was the first time white Americans were tried for killing Native Americans.

JESSAMYN WEST ▶

Facts-at-a-Glance

Nickname: The Hoosier State
Song: "On the Banks of the Wabash, Far Away"
Motto: The Crossroads of America
Flower: peony
Tree: tulip poplar
Bird: cardinal

Population: 5,544,000*
Rank in population, nationwide: 14th
Area: 36,420 sq mi (94,328 sq km)
Rank in area, nationwide: 38th
Date and ranking of statehood:
   December 11, 1816, the 19th state
Capital: Indianapolis
Major cities (and populations*):
   Indianapolis (731,300), Fort Wayne (173,000), Gary (116,650), Evansville (126,270), South Bend (105,510), Hammond (84,240), Muncie (72,600)
U.S. senators: 2
U.S. representatives: 10
Electoral votes: 12

*1990 Census.

66

Places to visit: Wyandotte Cave near Leavenworth, Brown County in south central Indiana, Indianapolis Motor Speedway, Children's Museum of Indianapolis, Levi Coffin House in Fountain City, Indiana Dunes National Lakeshore between Gary and Michigan City

Annual events: High School Basketball Tournament in Indianapolis (March), Spring Blossom Festival in Nashville (April), Bill Monroe's Bluegrass Festival in Beanblossom (June), Parke County Covered Bridge Festival (Oct.), Christmas at Conner Prairie Pioneer Settlement near Noblesville (Dec.)

Natural resources: soil, soft coal, clay, limestone, sand, gravel, natural gas, petroleum, peat

Agricultural products: corn, soybeans, hay, wheat, tobacco, tomatoes, cucumbers, snap beans, apples, hogs, milk, eggs

Manufactured goods: car and truck parts, televisions, steel, medicines, food products, chemicals, recreational vehicles

ENDANGERED SPECIES
Mammals—bobcat, gray bat, Indiana bat, evening bat, swamp rabbit
Birds—black-crowned night heron, barn owl, golden-winged warbler, sandhill crane
Amphibians and Reptiles—hellbender, hieroglyphic turtle, northern red salamander
Fish—bluebreast darter, Tippecanoe darter
Plants—hooded ladies' tresses, nodding trillium, spreading panic grass, pipewort

WHERE HOOSIERS WORK
Services—50 percent
  (services include jobs in trade; community, social, & personal services; finance, insurance, & real estate; transportation, communication, & utilities)
Manufacturing—26 percent
Government—15 percent
Agriculture—5 percent
Construction—4 percent

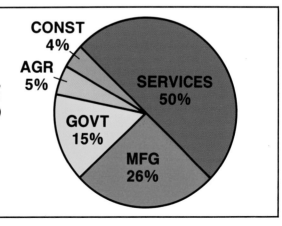

CONST
4%
AGR
5%
GOVT
15%
SERVICES
50%
MFG
26%

PRONUNCIATION GUIDE

Hoosier (HOO-zhur)

Lafayette (lawf-ee-EHT)

La Salle (luh SAL)

Maxinkuckee (mak-sin-KUHK-ee)

Oolotic (oo-LIHT-ihk)

Ouiatenon (WEE-a-teh-nahn)

Potawatomi
(paht-uh-WAHT-uh-mee)

Shawnee (shaw-NEE)

Tecumseh (tuh-KUHMP-suh)

Tenskwatawa
(ten-SKWAHT-uh-wah)

Terre Haute (ter-uh HOHT)

Tippecanoe (tip-ee-kuh-NOO)

Wyandotte (WY-uhn-daht)

Glossary

colony A territory ruled by a country some distance away.

constitution The system of basic laws or rules of a government, society, or organization. The document in which these laws or rules are written.

glacier A large body of ice and snow that moves slowly over land.

ice age A period when glaciers cover large regions of the earth. The term *Ice Age* usually refers to the most recent one, called the Pleistocene, which began almost 2 million years ago and ended about 10,000 years ago.

immigrant A person who moves to a foreign country and settles there.

landfill A place specially prepared for burying solid waste.

moraine A mass of sand, gravel, rocks, etc., pushed along or left behind by a glacier.

plantation A large estate, usually in a warm climate, on which crops are grown by workers who live on the estate. In the past, plantation owners often used slave labor.

reservation Public land set aside by the government to be used by Native Americans.

till A rich mixture of clay, sand, and gravel dragged along by a glacier and left behind when the ice melts.

Index

70

Acknowledgments:

Maryland Cartographics, Inc., pp. 2, 10; © (1992) Daniel Dempster, pp. 2, 6, 11, 59; Jack Lindstrom, p. 7; Richard Fields—Indiana DNR, pp. 8, 9, 12, 18, 57, 68; Indiana Farm Bureau, Inc., pp. 13, 47 (top right), 71; © (1992) Adam Jones, pp. 14, 15; Maslowski Photo, Cover, p. 16; J. Madeley/Root Resources, p. 17; Evansville Convention & Visitors Bureau, p. 20; Indiana Historical Society Library, pp. 22 (neg.#C5188), 28 (neg. #3288), 29 (neg. #B17), 30 (neg. #C2375), 32 (neg. #C5187); Paul L. Meyers/Root Resources, p. 23; Culver Pictures, Inc., p. 25; Tippecanoe County Historical Association, Lafayette, Indiana. Gift of Mrs. Cable G. Ball, p. 27; National Park Service, Lincoln Boyhood National Memorial, p. 31; Indiana Historical Society, pp. 33, 62 (middle left); Calumet Regional Archives, Indiana University Northwest, pp. 34, 56 (both); Library of Congress, p. 35; *Indianapolis News,* p. 36 (top); Indiana State Library, Indiana Division, pp. 37, 38, 39, 62 (top), 63 (bottom right), 65 (bottom right); Steven Purcell, The White House, p. 41; Indianapolis Convention & Visitors Association, pp. 42, 52 (right); Ed Hansen, pp. 43, 45 (both), 47 (bottom left); Root Resources, p. 44; Eli Lilly and Company, Indianapolis, Indiana, p. 46; Indianapolis Motor Speedway/Sam Scott, p. 48; I.U. Athletic Department Photo Lab, p. 49; Photograph by *Indianapolis Recorder*/Indiana Historical Society Library, p. 50 (neg. no. C5206); Anderson Visitors Bureau, p. 51; Jeff Greenberg, p. 52 (left); The Children's Museum of Indianapolis, p. 53; Peter Pearson/Root Resources, p. 54; Christanne Traxler, p. 58; *Du Pont Magazine,* p. 60; Earl L. Kubis/Root Resources, p. 61; Office of the Mayor, Gary, Indiana, p. 62 (middle right); AP/Wide World Photos, p. 62 (bottom); Dale Wittner, p. 63 (top); Hollywood Book & Poster, pp. 63 (far right), 64 (top); Twyla Tharp Dance Foundation, p. 63 (middle); Rudy Winston, p. 63 (bottom left); Army Signal Corps, National Archives, p. 64 (upper right); Duncan P. Schiedt, p. 64 (bottom right); Gary Gershoff/Retna Ltd., 65 (top); USIA, National Archives, p. 65 (bottom left); Jean Matheny, p. 66.

72